LOOK ON THE BRIGHT SIDE

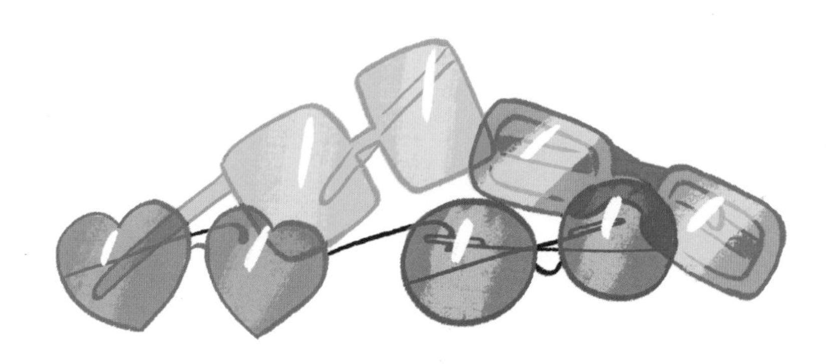

LOOK ON THE BRIGHT SIDE

Lily Williams &
Karen Schneemann

First Second
New York

The Mean Magenta

A blog about menstruation. Period.

Hello Mean Magenta Readers,

Long time no talk!

I took a break from my blog for the summer so I could relax. I had so much fun! I got thoroughly sunburned at the beach on a cloudy day and even got some summer freckles. I love my freckles, but ouch! Wear sunblock, people.

Christine, Sasha, and Brit have been busy with their advanced classes, which means they all have had summer study groups and homework. I haven't...but I'm not complaining since it's given me more time to work on my art.

I want to catch you up on last year though! We ended our sophomore year with a bang by getting enough menstrual supplies donated to our school to last through the upcoming year!! Then the school district agreed, thanks to our petition (and maybe my disruption—don't worry, I served my time in suspension), that they would budget in enough supplies to keep the girls' bathrooms stocked from here on out. I can't believe it! It's such a huge win for menstrual equity and we are all so happy!

There's more to do though and I have lots of ideas. Stay tuned and stay reading for more to come!

XO,
Abby

2 views

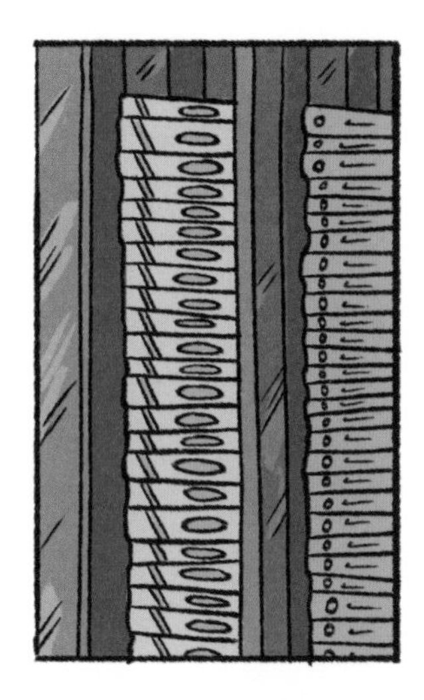

DONATED
MENSTRUAL
PRODUCTS
(USE FIRST)

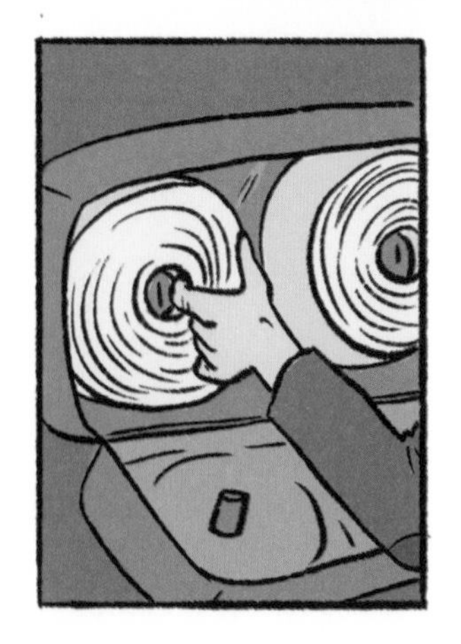

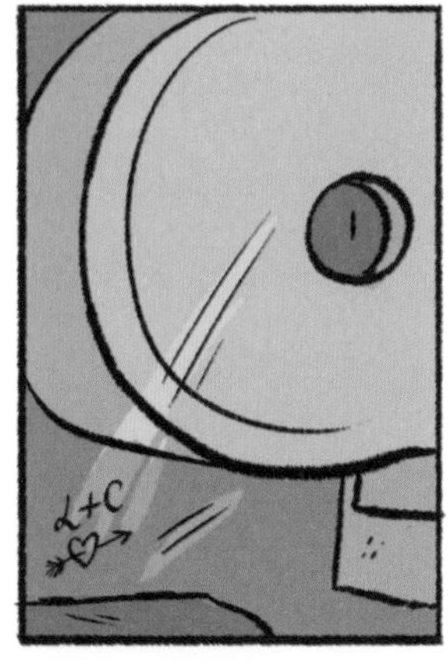
L+C

FREE

I don't understand.

I-I love you.
Most ardently.

* Sigh *

Feel
bette
endometri-go
away!
get
better
soon
Rx

SCREECH!
THUD
Ugh!
Close one.

TOSS

Click

ART

The Mean Magenta
Statistics

click
clack
Clack
Click
Type
Type

delete
delete
delete

SLAM

To: Tom

Scroll Scroll

What is it like
to be so in love
with you
Only I would be
so lucky to
know-ow-ow

It would hurt if I poked your tummy, right?

Oh my GOD. Yes. Don't you dare!

I wanna hear about it. Give me the deets about the blood and guts!
crunch

I promise I'll do the whole gross rundown. Let's just wait for Sash and Abby to get here first.

Speaking of Abs...
flip

I should probably tell her... huh?

That you have a big fat crush on her?

Yeah, I think that would probably be a good idea. At some point you're going to have to do it, or it will destroy you.

I think I'll just suffer forever since you're the only one who knows...that...
Well, you know.

You're right. Suffering in silence has always been the best, most effective way of dealing with something difficult.

SIGH

Ha ha.

Heh. I know...

Speaking of crushes...

Say what now? Don't tell me you have a crush on your lady doctor.
No.
You know that guy I told you about?

The barista from... Déjà Brew.

What about that guy in your English class you keep telling us about?

Fitz?
No, no. He's the worst—arrogant and rude and always correcting me in study group. He's barely tolerable.

Some could say the same thing about Ab—

Hi!

Abby!!

TOSS

!

Yes?

Nothing.

Flowers are from Mom and me.
So sweet. Thank you.

Hi! Hi! How's your tummy?

It's been better.

Wanna see my gnarly incisions?

Duh.
No.
Yes.

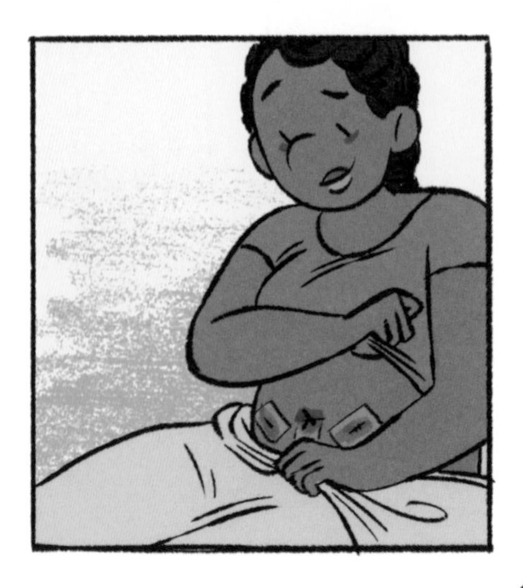

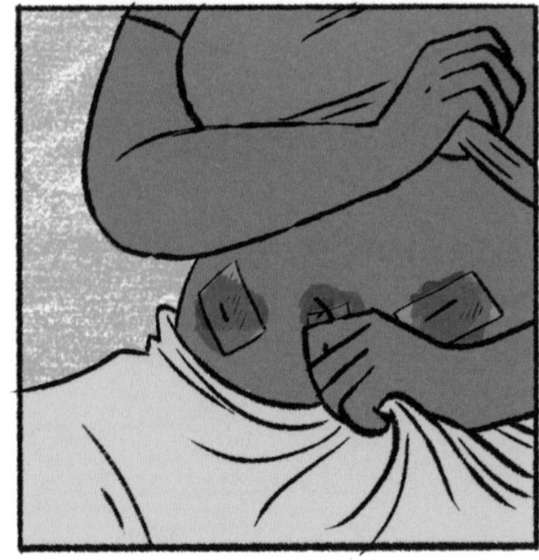

I'd say it looks worse than it feels, but they found endometriosis all over my bowels and uterus, and also a few fibroids on my uterus.
But my doctor didn't burn them—he cut the endometriosis cells out.
stomach
uterus
fibroids
cervix
vagina
large intestine
Which means they probably won't come back.
robotic tool
endometriosis
cut out at the root
I hope!

Pretty gnarly.

What stage were you?
Did they think you had adenomyosis?

What's that?
It's when the tissue like the stuff in your uterus grows *inside* your uterus muscles. Endo means it's growing *outside* the uterus.

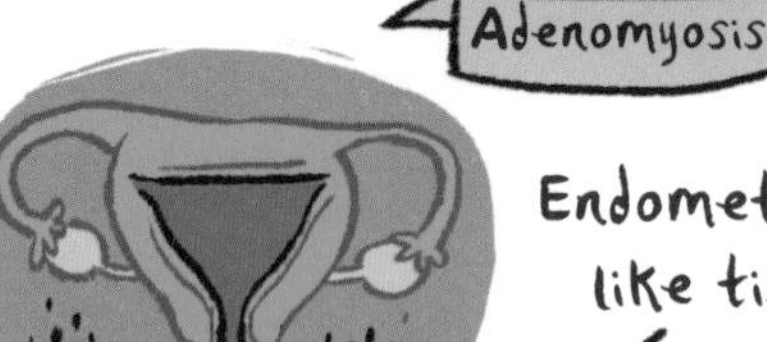
Adenomyosis

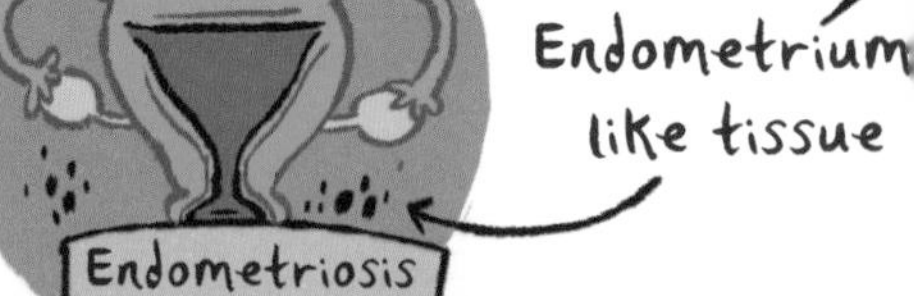
Endometrium like tissue
Endometriosis

Both sound awful.

nod

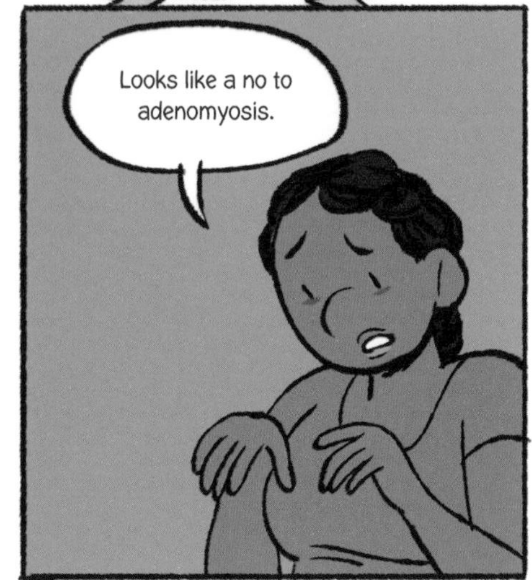
Looks like a no to adenomyosis.

But the endo and fibroids were confirmed and removed.

Wait, what's a fibroid?

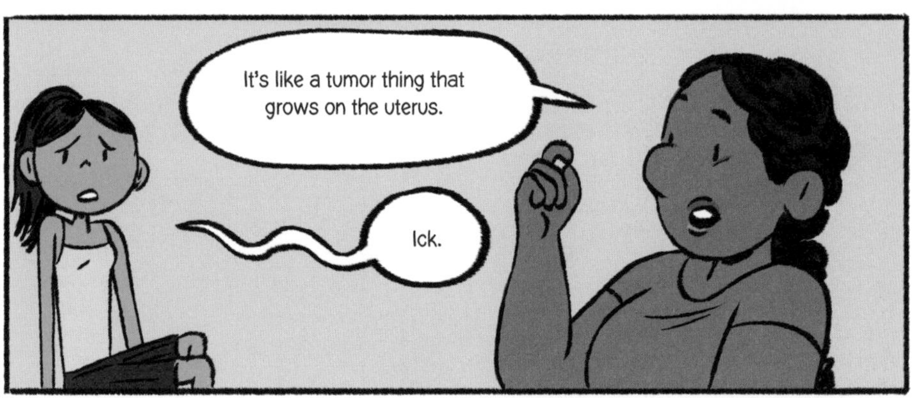
It's like a tumor thing that grows on the uterus.
Ick.

So are you totally cured, then?

Alas, they can't cure it, only cut it out. But hopefully it won't come back.

Tragic!

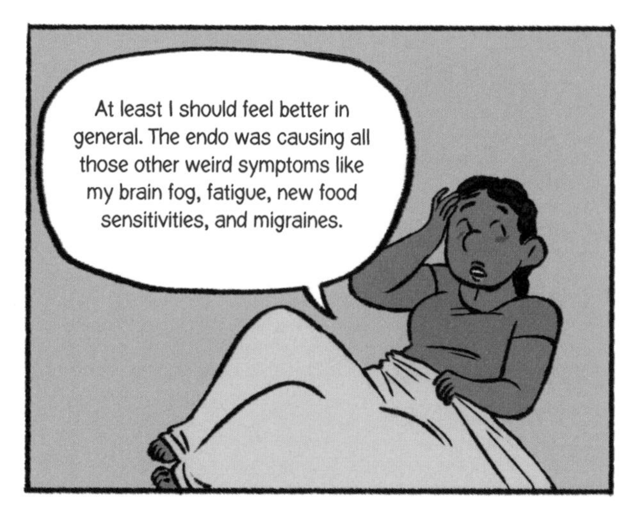
At least I should feel better in general. The endo was causing all those other weird symptoms like my brain fog, fatigue, new food sensitivities, and migraines.

It's so messed up that they literally had to cut you open to prove you had these things.
Seriously?! Couldn't they, like...just scan you?

Or listen in the first place.

Bzzzz! That's so brutal!

That seems like how they would diagnose you in ancient times, like the fifties or something.

The fifties weren't ancient times.
Says you.

ha ha ha

So now what?
Now I just keep resting for a few weeks, then I start pelvic physical therapy for a bit.

What does that entail? Pelvic PT...

You don't want to know.

If it's gross, don't tell me. I can only handle so much here.

It's okay, Sasha.

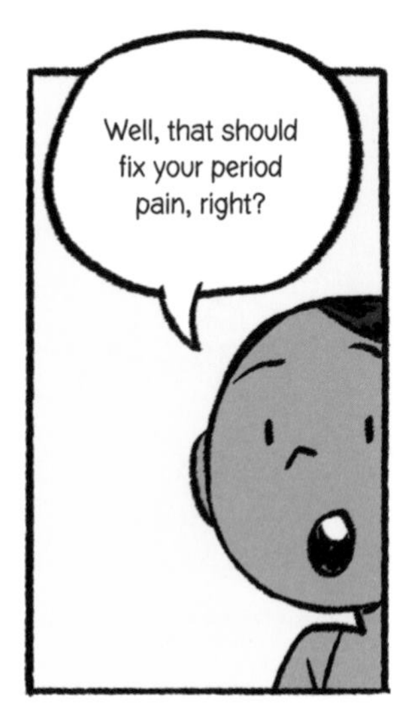
Well, that should fix your period pain, right?

Yeah, it should be a lot better now with some birth control to help regulate the hormones.

At least you're going to get them! I haven't gotten a period in months.

You're making me jealous here.

No, I promise my way is weird too... It's like...what are these small boobs? I want bigger ones. I want a regular period!
Ugh, I'm sorry.

ha ha ha

Hey, if it makes you feel any better, Christine has little boobs too!

Hey, I bleed every thirty days on the dot—don't come for me!
Want to trade, then?

I'll give you some of my boobs if you want.
Ditto...but no surgery for a while for me again.

Maybe one day my body will catch up with my superior intellect.

wink

Just grow two more feet to catch up with me, then you can tower over everyone.

RAWR!
ha ha ha

Abby, please write a blog post about endometriosis, then write one about my lack of periods. Thank you.

I'll get on it.

You haven't posted in a while. I check every day.

You do?

Someone's gotta give you your one page view a day.

thud

Hey, don't throw Lady Catherine de Bourgh!

Lady Catherine de Whatnow?

ha ha ha ha ha

Tuesday,
August 10th

Uh, hi.

Is Brit home?

Maybe. What's it to you?

I'm Fitz. I'm in Brit's AP English class, and we have our summer study group... Can you give her our notes from our last meeting?

I could, or I could go back to watching TV.

Here.

drop
Make an effort, please.

Nice car!

SLAM
From some grumpy dude for Brit.
I liked him.

Two hours later
DING DONG

Who are you?

Jorge. And who are you?

Lydie.

I heard Brit had surgery. Can you give these to her?

This is way better than that dumb stack of homework the other guy brought.

Other guy?

Yeah.

Tell Brit they're from Jorge and that I hope she feels better.
Okay.

. . .

Bye.

Some dude brought these.
feel better

PLUNK

That's my wat—

Wait, what
dude?

Uh...he
had, like,
a camo
shirt on...

Jorge?

SNAPS
Yeah, him. Much
cooler than the guy
from earlier.

SWIPE

Brit:
Jorge just brought
me flowers!
Sasha:
STOP!!!

Christine:
Grumpy one
from study group?
Brit:
No, the cute one
from Déjà Brew
down the street.

type
type
type

Lydie! Stop.

Can I at least have some
flowers for my troubles?

What troubles?

PUNCH
Maybe you haven't noticed, but I'm fending off your male suitors right now.

Fine.

SNAP
Send picture

Wednesday, August 11th

I want to make varsity this year.
We're both juniors, so I think it's a lock for us now.

It's a miracle I can run so fast for being so small.

Are you kidding me? Size does *not* determine speed. Cheetahs aren't very big and they're the fastest.
I guess...

I mean, think what that would mean for elephants. Wait.
On second thought...
That sounds like the stuff of nightmares. I would not want an elephant coming at me with the speed of a cheetah.
ha ha ha
True.

You gotta stop undercutting yourself, dude.

How are you so confident?
I wish I didn't let things bother me so much. You're so casual about everything. You, like...swagger.

Hah!
Yeah. Right. Me?
I'm serious. How do you do it?

Well...

I guess it's easy. It's all about using humor to cover up traumatic things... like the stuff with my mom.

Or so said the therapist Gram sent me to.
Before I quit.

Maybe you could go back.

I don't know why.
It's not like being closeted is—

UHHH.

Does Gram know?
Uhhh...not exactly.
I figured. It's cool.

Don't worry. I won't say anything.

Thanks.

Still she/her pronouns?
I think so, yeah.

I'll let you know
if it changes.
Okay, cool.

I'm here
for you.

Thank you,
Little Cheetah.

ha
ha
ha

Later that night
BRUH.

SWIPE

SWIPE

SWIPE

toss

sSSIGHHHHHH

BRUH.

Friday, August 13th

Thanks for walking with me, guys. It's way more fun doing these daily walks with other people.

Doesn't Lydie come sometimes?
Yeah, but she gets bored with how slow I am right now.

Sounds about right.

I wish I had a sibling. I think they would be like a built-in best friend.
Are you kidding? My brother hates me.
ha ha ha

No, I'm not kidding. I don't have anyone.

Gram is wonderful. What are you talking about?
Yeah, but Gram's old. She's not going to run or swim with me.

She can't keep up with this beast.

I can't keep up with Lydie!

I think you're being very optimistic about this. My brother farts on my head when he tackles me and always reminds me what a stupid shrimp I am. We have to share everything and I swear my parents always side with him...
nods

Built-in people who love you no matter what.

Just being related to someone doesn't mean that you're going to agree with them or even love them.

There's someone always there for you though.

Are you saying we aren't there for you?

No, no, you are!

I'm just saying, doesn't it mean more that your friends *choose* to be around you?

Like you know those friends are there for you because they want to be.
It's a choice to be there for someone you love instead of just needing to be there because you're related.

BUT! What if I want to fart on someone's head.
Don't you dare fart on my head.

Okay, bad example.

But what if I do something and you guys just leave.

Why would we leave?
It happens...

That's family, right? Now you're arguing my whole point.
Shut up.

Anyone can leave at any time, but the friends you choose and the ones who choose to be with you are there because they love you.
Isn't that love just as valuable?

...

eyes darting

I've never seen Christine speechless.

You're good at arguing.
flip
Thank you. I got a lot of practice from my brother.

Saturday,
August 14th

KATIE

Ughhh!
What "ugh"?

This doesn't look like the history paper you said you were writing.

My stats are so bad now.

What do you mean?

I see my one page view a day is going strong.

SLAM

I don't care about being famous.
SLIP

I don't care about trending. I don't care about going viral. I just feel like I'm burning out.
I never know what to write about anymore, and when I do make a blog post, you're the only one who reads it.

And your mom.
And my mom.
I want the world to be kinder and better. I just don't even know where to start.
I know.
SLIPPING

Let's just ignore the world for now and pick your outfit for the first day of school.

I'm thinking laid-back but, like... cute.

Do I not do that already?

ha ha ha

Don't you want to look cute in case...

...anyone missed you over the summer?

Fine, tell me
what you think
I'd look cute in.

Eee! Fun!

Okay... I'm
thinking...

Tuesday, August 17th

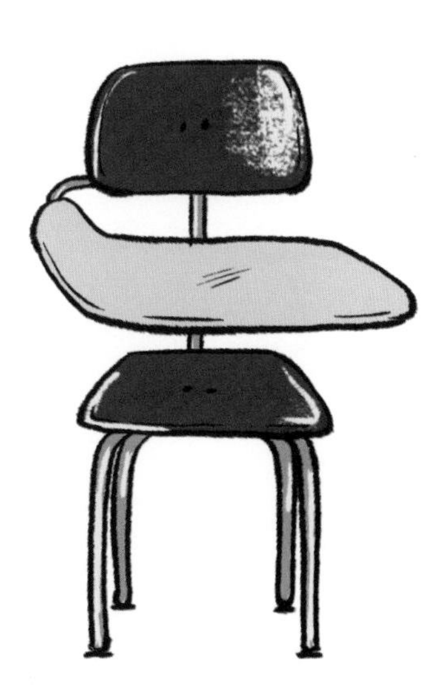

RING
RING
RING
RING

Pick your seats, students. These will be your seats...

...for the rest of the year.
SLAM

Look who it is! I didn't know you were in this class.
WINK
Why are you surprised? Don't you know I'm both beauty and brains, Brit?

SCOFF

As you all should know now, I'm Mr. Collins. This is AP English.

A.P. ENGLIS
GR
Everyone, pull out your notes from your summer reading.

We are jumping in right away.

Now, what would we say our biggest themes are in *Great Expectations*?

Do you have your notes from summer reading?

I'm a little behind.

Uh...

Sure.
Fitzgerald & Brit
AP English
Mr. Collins

You're the best.

Wednesday,
August 25th
CALCULUS

...anyway, that's the end of that.

Tom's having me try jelly babies after practice.
huff
huff

We've been on this "he tries American food, I try British food" thing.

What in the Cheez Whiz is a jelly baby?

Do they eat babies in England?

Heh heh, I don't know, actually.
I'm pretty sure they're some kind of candy...? But he's excited about them...

So I guess I am too.

Being a couple sounds weird. I'm not ready for jelly babies.

ha
ha ha
ha
ha

We're, like, four days into school, and haven't you gone to Tom's every day after practice?
Uh, yeah. Why?

Are you guys studying together?

Or are the jelly babies doing your homework for you?

It's just the first week, Christine.
We don't even have that much homework.

Speak for yourself. I have, like, a butt ton of pre-calc.
Ew. No.

whispers
Have you talked to Abby?

Play it cool, man. Not at school.

Sorry.

Thursday, August 26th

The principal will see you now, Abby.
Go in, sweetie.

Oh. You're not Mr. Westin.

I'm not.

I'm Ms. Henderson.

I'm Abby Sinclair, and last year I got the district to agree to put free pads and tampons in the girls' bathrooms after an initiative where "technically" I got suspended, but also I crowdfunded resources to start the process.

I've heard about you, and I'm excited to hear what ideas you have. I'm assuming that's why you're here.
Uh...yes.

Ahem. I want Hazelton to become even more inclusive for all people and provide menstrual products in all the bathrooms. I want this because I want Hazelton to be a safe place for everyone who menstruates regardless of gender. Trans, genderqueer, and nonbinary students all deserve to feel included here, and access to period products is an affordable way to make this clear.

We're on the same page. I've been thinking along those lines, and I want to see what we can do.

Really?

Yeah, in fact it's already being discussed by some members of the LGBTQIA+ club.

The president came and talked to me about it last week.

Wow.

Do you know about it? They call themselves the Unicorn Club.

THE HAZELTON HIGH
Unicorns
LGBTQIA+ CL
THURSDAYS
everyone's welcome!
ROOM 303
Can anyone be part of it?
The club is for anyone who wants to join, and you might find some like-minded people and allies there.

Today is Thursday.

I think if we got enough people with the passion you all have shown me, we can build good momentum to make changes for our Hazelton High Hazlenuts!

I like that.
Maybe you can write a proposal for me about why this is important so I can use student voices to help the district understand.

Okay.

Why don't you try to make the Unicorn Club right now before they finish?

I will. Thank you,
Ms. Henderson.

30

Hi! Here for the
Unicorn Club meeting?
SLAM

Um, yes. I think so.

Since we already all know each other, you can introduce yourself last so you can see how we do things.

Hi! I'm Thalia, and I'm a senior. I'm pansexual, and my favorite thing I did this summer was white water rafting!

Hi, I'm Bryce, and I'm in tenth grade. I got a few new light sticks this summer and went to see my favorite K-pop band live.
It was amazing.

Um, hi. I'm Fitzgerald. You can call me Fitz. I, um, am in eleventh grade, and I'm here because my brother came out as trans this summer, and I want to be a better big brother.
Nice!

Hi, so, right. I'm Abby.
A junior.
And, um, I'm not really sure why I'm here.
I guess I want to learn?

Learning is a great reason to be here!

Okay, everyone, the bell is about to ring. We have some cool things to talk about, so I hope to see everyone next week!

Hi.

See you next week.
Okay.
RING
RING
RING

Tuesday,
August 31st

CLICK

CLICK

Will you quit it? You're making me nervous.

Literally, Christine, if you're going to be such a whiny butt about, uh...
STANDS

whispers
...Abby.

Then you need to talk to her. I can't survive your moodiness.

Don't get me wrong.
I, like, love you expressing your emotions, but you've been talking in circles a lot lately and have been grumpier than usual.

Uggggggggghh
hhhhhhhhhhhhhh
hhhhhhhhhhhhh

Fine. But how in the Nutter Butter am I supposed to even do that...

Hi, I think you're cute...

and your red hair is cute...
and your smile is cute and I really want to smile at you more and have you smile at me more.
So what do you think,
Ab—

Let's make a code name for safety.

Little Mermaid.
You're kidding.

JUMPS
It's **PERFECT!**

Chen, no jumping near the vials.
Oops.

Little Mermaid might like you back, but you won't ever know until you're honest.

But being honest means saying the g-word and then saying the *like* word and then...

That's too many words.
Really, you just mentioned two words.

I mean, I know this is probably really hard...but Ariel is the most understanding person, if not a really intense person.
What if she feels just as intensely about you or something?

She's right. You couldn't have picked a more passionate...mermaid.
NODS

But what if she doesn't even like girls?

Or worse, what if she's passionately against me?
SNORTS

But what if you have no idea what she's thinking? What if you need to talk to her to find out how she feels?

I'm going to grab her in the hallway and maybe...
RING
RING
RING
Glasses still on, Sasha!

Oh.

Excuse me.

Oops.
BUMP
Excuse you.

Where did you come from?

AP Chemistry.

I wish I was in the smart people classes with you all.

Hey, I was wondering if I could talk to you about something.
Always.

It's been, like, a while coming, but I was thinking I should let you know...
Huh?

Well, that is to say I...

You've been keeping a secret from me, you poop!

Oh no! I would...
never...
It's just that it's been forever since I figured things out...
And I...

You're concerning me.

HA HA HA HA HA HA HA HA HA

I think you should know I think you're really smart. Even if you're not in our classes.

Oh, thanks.
I don't feel smart today. I just got a C on a test.

Oh no, really?

Well, tests are for nerds.

I mean, kinda true.

ha ha ha

Whoa, look at that squirrel up there!

SLICE

I don't see it.

Must have flown away.
What?

Nothing happened **today** or *ever.*
Oh look, an apple.
I love apples.

You're acting weirder than normal today,
and that's a pretty high bar for you.

Oh, Gram.
Is that from Easter?

Friday, September 3rd

Ap English

Well, clearly they're using soma to control the population, but what do we think this echoes in our world today?
I think we could look at it from a lot of different angles.

For instance you could see it being both pro- and anti-communism, depending on how you look at—
Brit, can you do a summary first, to get us caught up?

Presumably we are caught up if we've done the reading.
Presumably.
I just wanna hear how Brit interpreted it.

It doesn't matter how Brit interpreted it.

Wow.
Fitz. Yes it does.

Well, it shouldn't. We should all have done the work, and if you didn't, that's not Brit's problem to solve.

I'm just saying I want to hear what Brit has to say. She's always got good answers.

I don't always have good answers.

You're, like, the smartest person in the class.
BUMP
Okay, I can summarize.

So...

Saturday,
September 4th

I don't need backups,
I'm going to Harvard.

nods
I'll be right back. You don't need to pause it.

POPCORN

POP
POP
POPCORN
POP

Finished with your homework tonight?
Uh, yup.
POP
POP POP

It doesn't seem like you've had a lot of homework this year so far.
Yeah, I thought you were in advanced classes, Sasha.
I am. I guess it's a bit easier this year.
POP POP POP POP POP POP POP POP POP POP

When Tyler was a junior, he had so much homework, and he would be so tired after lacrosse practice that he would fall asleep on his desk.

POP
POP
POP
Oh, that's funny. Maybe I'm in advanced classes for dummies or something. I haven't really had that problem.

You've been really hard on yourself lately. Are you feeling okay? He's still being nice to you, right?

Mom. Tom is stinking wonderful, as usual.
eye roll
Don't worry... I'm fine. It's just...
I don't really know what it is.

Be kind to yourself, my little bunny.
KISS
POP
POP
POP

gasp
BEEP

POPCORN

Why don't you just check for your dear old dad that you got all of your work done.

Okay, I'll double-check.

Hey, Sasha.

Yeah?

You know we're proud of you, right?
Mom...

You can do anything you set your mind to, Sasha. I really believe that.
But...

...But?

But you've got to put in the work. A lot of good things in life are hard. You have to work for them. They don't just land in your lap, no matter how cute you are.
Okay, Mom. I get it.
You could do anything, like Elena Woods in that movie you like. Or that Miss Funny Lady in the beauty pageant.
Elle Woods and Miss Congeniality?

Yeah, them. They worked hard in high school and got good jobs.

I don't think that's the point of those movies.
Well whatever it is, consider yourself parented. Now go watch the rest of your movie.

Everything okay?
Yeah, it's fine.

Sasha, you're such a stupid little dork.
You got into Harvard Law?
What, like it's hard?

Wednesday,
September 8th

In a single paragraph, how could one argue that soma is both good and bad for the population?
I'm going to ace this!
Pssst!
Points

shakes head

pouts

mouthing
Number two?

SHAKES HEAD

COUGH
KICK

teeth gritted
Stop.

Everything all right over there?
It's fine.
Oh, I just got so into this test that I got a hand cramp. I think I need a water break.

If it's not life or death, let's save it until after the test is finished.

flip

Thursday, September 9th

Hey, before Christine gets here...
does it seem like she's been acting weird lately?

I keep thinking maybe I said something to her and she's mad at me?

It almost feels like she's hiding something...

Or the most wild thought is, like...maybe she's gay and doesn't think I'd accept her or something? She's never said anything to me about it, but I've always wondered...
Um...

Does she think we wouldn't love her? Or maybe she really is mad at me...
She keeps acting like she has something to tell me but never does.

I have an idea... Why don't you just ask her what seems to be bothering her? You guys are so close.

Yeah, you're right.

Hellooooo howdy.

swallows

Sasha, you ready for that quiz after lunch?
What quiz?!

The one in French.
. . .

Ugh, what an idiot. *God*, what is wrong with me?

Sasha, you'll do fine. It's just the stuff on last week's homework.
Yeah...that's not going to help me.

I've talked to the principal about getting pads and tampons in all the bathrooms so the school is more inclusive.

Rad.
She wants me to draft a formal proposal to bring to the district. I seriously don't even know where to start!

Oh yeah?

Abby, you should talk to this guy in my English class. His name is Fitz.

He's a really good writer.
Oh! I know him!

Really?
Do you
have
classes
together?

I just met him at this...
thing. But okay,
maybe I'll ask him.

He's pretty grumpy,
but pretty smart.
Wait, Brit. Do you
have a crush?

On Fitz?!
You so do.
Look at you!

Hello!

Brit has a
secret crush on
some dude.

Do not!

Methinks the lady doth protest too much.

shrugs

Eh, who cares who thinks who is cute.

Sunday,
September 12th

Your mom is stress-baking again.

I know. She has a show she's got to install next weekend and she's not ready.

Procratstination station.

Exactly.

You've got some... stuff on your face.

Oh.

wipe

Is it gone?

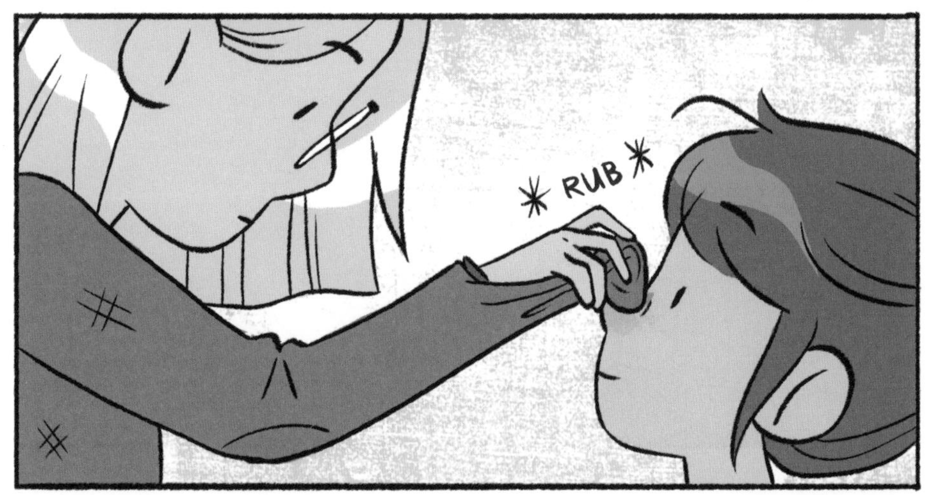
RUB

All gone.

So where's this algebra homework you're so frustrated with?

Oh, it's... well, it *was* right here...

Unicorn
Room 303

hides

See this whole chapter? I don't understand anything. We learned about it in class, but it just zoomed through my head.

Oh, rad. I love quadratic equations.

I don't understand how you understand math. It's a foreign language.

It kinda is...but I think my brain just works that way. I like knowing when I'm right.
I just hate second-guessing everything and all the... squishiness of not having one right answer. Besides, math is kinda fun.

Not fun.

You can pretend you're a pirate trying to find *X* and make it fun with your big ol' imagination brain. You're the most creative person I know! I'm sure you can make this fun, if you try.

ha ha ha

So, I've been wanting to ask you... Are you mad at me?

swallow

Why would you think that?

You've just not been hanging out with me that much, and you aren't looking at me, and I feel like I said something to upset you.
Did I?
I'd be super upset if I hurt you. I don't ever want to hurt you.

Noooo you couldn't.
You didn't.
What I mean to say is...

Oh god, I did something bad. I did, didn't I?

Slow down, Abs! It's just that I, well, you see...
I really like you, so I'd...

Phew. Gosh, I know. I like you too!

I was getting nervous we were growing apart or something and I just really want to be best friends forever.

QUACK
QUACK
QUACK
GRAM

QUACK
QUACK
QUACK

What's up, Gram?

Yeah, I can come home. It's no problem. See you soon.

I gotta go. I'll video chat you when I'm home and we can be pirates together.

ARGGG!

What?

Never mind.
Anyway.

To be continued...

???

shrugs
UGH.

Thursday,
September 23rd

jingle

You know, what if I just became a nun or something?
Are you even religious?

Jesus had some cool sandals I could be down with...

I certainly shouldn't be allowed to talk to crushes after last night. Nun it is!

I think that's extreme. But I support the Jesus thing if you want.

Isn't that the dude from your class?

gasp

tug

Why are we hiding?
Shhh!

whisper

I can't hear them. Can you?

No, I can't. Hmmm.

He seems grumperton as usual, Brit.

Why are they just ripping the posters down?

Maybe they hate the posters and whoever made them?
Those are Abby's posters.

WHY I OUGHTA!!

Let's just leave. I don't want to deal with this right now.
Jesus would not approve.
You're on your way to nunhood.
I don't think that's what it's called.

Friday, October 1st

RING
RING

What's up, Sasha?
swipe

SOBBING
Sasha?
Brit… I got my progress report card and I've got all Cs.

Whoa. How did that happen?
I don't know.
SOB
I don't know.

Oh, Sasha.

I'm so dumb. I got so infatuated with a boy that I let everything go and it piled up so quickly.

SOB
SOB
gasp
Breathe.

Sasha!
I hate myself.
I hate who I am.
Take a deep breath, girl. Why are you being so mean to yourself?
inhale
Because I deserve it. I did this to myself.
That's ridiculous! Imagine if Tom could hear you. He would tell you to love yourself.
You need to talk to yourself how you would talk to me.

What would you say to me if I was getting Cs?

You're right.

It's only midsemester. We can fix this.
We can? Are you sure??

We can and we will. You don't have to do this alone.
Okay.

Did Elle Woods do it alone?

No, she didn't. She had her friends.

You're going to set a timer for forty-five minutes and do your English homework and nothing else. When it goes off, you have a bite of chocolate.

Thanks, Brit.

Go get 'em!

50%

Later that night...

I just can't believe I let my grades slip that far.

I just wish you'd told me you weren't doing your homework all those times we hung out... I wouldn't have wanted to hang out if I knew you weren't.
I know, and that's part of why I didn't tell you. I just wanted to have fun.

We will still have fun. But maybe we'll schedule more study dates.

Okay, great! I've been thinking lately...that I might want to be a lawyer. Like Elle Woods.
Really? I'd be chuffed to be with a lawyer.

You would??

Wait. "Chuffed" is a good thing, right?

Ha ha, yep. You'd be a brilliant lawyer. You really know how to win an argument with me!
Thanks, sweets.

What can I do to help get your grades up? I can't really help you study because you're in higher classes than I am.

I think I just need to make some boundaries...like maybe we can only hang out on weekends. Are you mad if I ask that? I think you're too...distracting.

I respect that. I am a bit more interesting than pre-calc.

Cool.

Wednesday,
October 13th

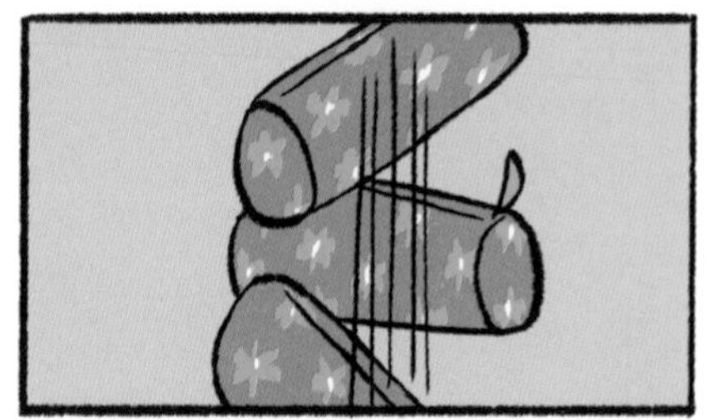

* Swipe *

I got it! Here ya go.

Oh hey, Jorge!

I'm actually glad I ran into you.

I hope you're not mad at me for bugging you during our English test the other day.

What? Oh no!
Of course not!
I was just... super focused. You know?

Cool. Yeah. I totally focus on stuff too.

Maybe you could help me prep for the next test. I'm *sooo* busy, you know?

And you're so good at this reading and writing stuff.

You think?

Totally. That guy Fitz is such a jerk though.

I think he was trying to get me in trouble or something.

Uh...yeah. Maybe. I mean, he can be pretty condescending sometimes.
Right? He thinks he's smarter than everyone.

ha
ha
ha

You know, the other day I saw him tear down my friend Abby's posters. She worked really hard on them.

People can be so judgmental and totally uncool. You know?

What about my posters?

Anyways, catch ya later.

Hey, Abs.

Hey. So... what?

Who tore my posters down?
That guy Fitz from my English class.

Fitz? Curly-haired Fitz?
He's probably just jealous you're out there changing the world.

I guess I'm just surprised because I talk to him sometimes.
I didn't realize you talked that often.

Yeah, in this club. I just don't think he'd do that. He's... sensitive.

Well, either way, I think your posters are a good idea.
Yeah, me too.

Friday, October 15th

Unicorn Club meeting
CHAMPION
unicorns
YOU CAN DO IT!

I guess I think it's weird people are so worried about how other people identify instead of just... helping them feel better.

I thought your article in the school paper did a good job of laying out why we all need menstrual products.

I worry about that with my brother. When he gets to Hazelton, I just want it to be a less judgmental place.

I think you're going to make it that way for him!

You've already started. I'm honored you asked me to help alongside the cool people here in this room.

You're clearly a good big brother.

I like that the principal is so responsive. Sounds much better than last year.
That's true, for sure.

Um. So this is a weird question, but are you sure you want to help me with this project?

What?

Well, someone said they saw you tearing down some of my posters and I wanted to ask you about it because...

we're working on this thing together and I kinda thought we'd become friends,

and I just want to make sure you actually want to help.

Abby, that's crazy. Of course I want to help!

I respect you a lot, and I respect what you're trying to do to make this school a more equitable place.
Okay, great.

Didn't you get my e-mail?
I took down some of the posters because I found a typo. Once we fix it, I'll definitely help you put them back up.

Wow, really?? I guess I haven't checked my e-mail lately. I can't say I'm surprised.

I'm such a bad speller. I probably need you to proofread everything I write!
It probably looked pretty bad if someone saw me tearing down those posters...

Yeah, when I overheard Brit and Jorge talking about it, I couldn't even wrap my head around it. Like, why would you even do that?
Brit and Jorge were the ones you heard it from?

That makes sense.
It does?

Jorge worked for my dad last summer, and when my brother came out and started to transition, Jorge just... was weird. My dad had to let him go, and he's been mad at me ever since.
I don't think it helps that we both...

Well, Brit has been a good English buddy.

Brit is a wonderful friend.
BUT—

But it's a huge CRUSH!

!!!

Then let him know.
Do you know how scary that is? When I see him, we're just the best of friends.

I know it doesn't matter if he's my best friend or if his sexuality aligns—that's just a societal construct, right? I guess you're right.

The only thing that matters is how you feel when you're around someone.

But then I started noticing this
growing tension around such
ridiculous, silly little things.

And then he started avoiding eye contact and acting differently.
Hey, before Christine gets here... does it seem like she's been acting weird lately?
Different how?
Just...different. Like at first I thought he was mad. Then he was just awkward.
To be continued...
When I think about what I want and who I want to date, it's never really clear.

But when I'm with him, I feel butterflies and always want to be by his side.
I love it.
His smile is so cute, and he's silly in all the right ways.
It just makes sense.

Is this the LGBT Club?
BAM
Come on in! We're just finishing up and free chatting since lunch is almost over.

glance
SLAM

wave
wave

Isn't that your friend Christine?

Oh...um, yeah.

RING
RING
RING
RING

hold

What were you doing there?

I want to learn.
Gram is gay.

What?

I need to get to the 200s wing, so gotta jet!

Sunday, October 24th

shake

Dang! I ran out of ink!

Really? You must be an insane writer! I honestly don't think I've ever had a pen run out of ink...

That's probably because you have so many! I doubt you use the same pen twice!

I've actually been eyeing those gel pens since I got here. Can I use one?

Like you even have to ask! Of course! Here, this kind is my fave. Green or blue?

Green—like Jorge's eyes!
Sigh
You're crushing *hard*, Brit. I've never seen you like this when you aren't watching some old Victorian romance.
Well, first of all, I usually prefer Regency to the Victorian era when it comes to historical romances.
rolls eyes
But I know it's kinda hard to believe someone as perfect as Jorge could exist at Hazelton.
Perfect? That's pretty intense. I don't think anyone's perfect... even Tom!
Well...I guess not. I mean, it would be nice if he put in more effort during class. And I guess he did go a little over the top insulting Fitz. He's not *that* bad.
Hey, that's right! Whatever happened to your crush on good ol' grumpy pants?

Pffft. I never had a crush on him, Sasha!
I can respect someone's intellect without falling in love with them.

Umm, if you say so...

Ugh. You're lucky that you found Tom and you guys are so good together. It's so easy for you! You don't have to try to figure out whether he likes you. It's so obvious!

It is kind of nice.

I really don't know how I lucked out and found someone so perfect.

I thought you said no one was perfect! Hypocrite!
Never mind what I said five minutes ago.

I live in the moment, and in this moment Tom is perfect!

0:12

Hey! I've still got three more math problems and our forty-five minutes is almost up! Get back to work!

Yes, ma'am.
Taking your reward early, I see...

I may have created a monster.

Wednesday, October 27th

Ugh!

Ugh!

UGH!

What are you grumping on about, lovely?

inhale

Would you still love me if I were different?

I love you now, don't I? You're pretty unique!

But what if it was something that wasn't so cool when you were a kid?
There was a lot that wasn't cool when I was a kid. Doesn't mean it was right.

What if I don't like boys?

Then you probably shouldn't date them.

Now that that's settled. Why don't I go see if we have any leftover lasagna in the freezer...
That sounds like a nice meal for the heart, doesn't it?
IES

DING DONG
KIE

DING
DONG

What are you—

Hi! We were on our way home and my mom wants that container back.
What container?

The one I brought over two months ago with the brownies? It's square and has some blue on it.

The one that's sitting on the table right there with the note on it that says "Abby."

Hi, Gram!

Just to clear the air, Christine told me, and I think it's really cool.
!!

?!
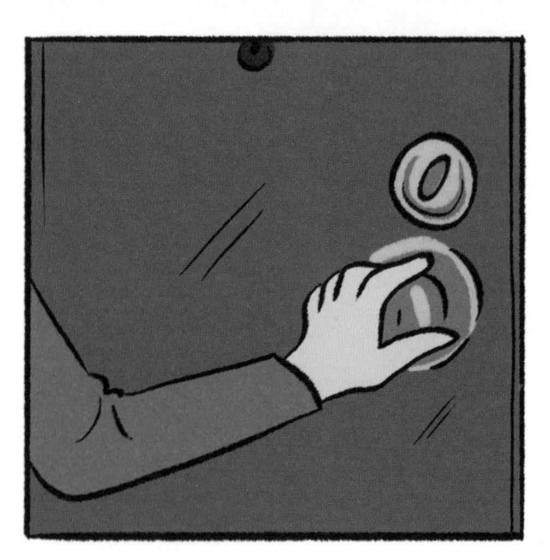

!!!
SHOVE

Bye, Gram. We support you!

See you tomorrow at school. I have homework.
SLAM

What was that?
Lasagna sounds great.

Wednesday,
November 3rd

gasp

Do you want to borrow mine? I have a hood, so I don't really need it.

No thanks. I think I have one in my locker.

Brit, wait.
Yeah?

I, uh...
You're smart.

Thank you? I think?

I like that. About you, I mean.

I guess I mean I like you.
And I was wondering if you wanted to go out sometime.

With me.

Look, Fitz...

Being smart and getting good grades isn't everything. If you want people to like you, you have to be nice to them. I'm sorry, but I can't date someone who doesn't respect my friends.

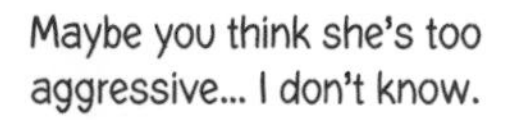
What?

I saw you tearing down Abby's posters.

Maybe you think she's too aggressive... I don't know.
But I can't believe you took down her posters.
She cares about these issues because she wants to change the world for the better. You only care about your grades and out-smarting kids in your class.
So I guess you couldn't understand why she's like that.

Maybe you should talk to your friends before accusing people of things. Maybe you'll be surprised at what you find.
You don't know anything about my friends. Or about me.

RUMB
You're just a clueless, privileged guy who doesn't understand or think about these issues.

Is that what you really think?
Thank you for being honest with me.

I won't bother you again.
See you in class.

exhale

toss

RUMBLE
VROOM

BEEP

3
DING
DONG

Whoa!

You're soaked.
Come in, come in.

Do you like Fitz?

Fitz...
gerald?
Yeah, Fitz.

ha ha ha ha ha ha ha ha ha ha ha

Oh my god,
no I don't!

Oh.

Wait...
do you?

I...I don't
know.
He just
told me he
liked me.
He just asked
me out!
But...I saw him tearing
down your posters.
I can't date
someone who's
just...just a jerk!

Oh, Brit.

I do not like Fitz.

And he's really not a jerk.
Did you know I spelled "inclusive" starting with an *e* on that poster?
BEEP

What? Like as a joke?

No! I'm bad at spelling and made a huge typo. Fitz caught it and took down the posters and e-mailed me so I could fix my mistake.

Oh... That's... really nice.

I should have told you but once he told me why he took them down, but I was just relieved and wanted to forget about the whole thing. I didn't want anyone to know.

Well, everyone makes typos.
Yeah, but that one is just so stupid and then I went and plastered it all over the school.

So, do you like Fitz?

Well, I don't know. I mean, he's smart and we get along in class.
He seems to be my friend, I think?
He's cute.
I like that he's so serious, but I think maybe that's just his outer layer.

Yeah, I think I feel that way about someone too.
But different, because my person isn't serious.

Really? Who?
They might actually be the opposite of serious.

Do I know them?

Mm-hmm.

Are you going to tell me more?
I don't know...
Not yet.

What if I also don't know where it's going or I don't want to put a label on it?

Can I just think someone is cute and want to kiss them? Is that allowed?

I think anything is allowed. I think people need to find their own way.
As long as you're not a jerk.

Ugh, I was a jerk.
Maybe a little, but it wasn't intentional!

You didn't have all the facts!

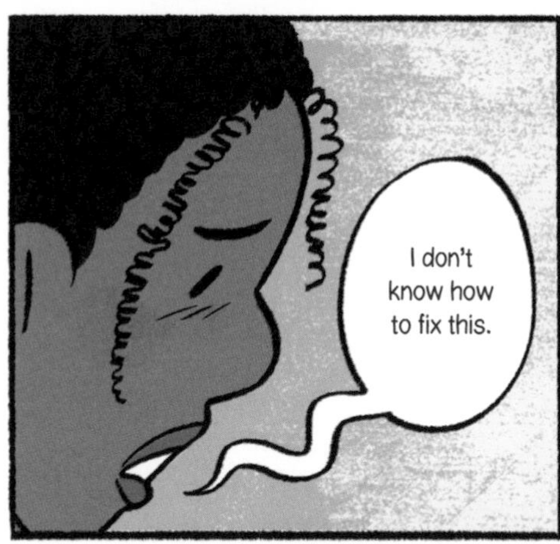
I don't know how to fix this.

We can fix this.

Thursday,
November 4th

I really am starting to get this now.
Only took a month of catch-up.

drop
Good for you.
Uh, what.
I think I'm going to drop out and become a hermit.

It will be easier if I just drop out. I want to talk to Abby, but if I ruin our whole friend group because of hormones...
...what is the ***POINT!***

Chris!

SOB

SOB
SOB
SOB
SOB

Christine, you need to live your life. You can't run and hide from something this important. And Abby is part of this for you right now.
I know.

Love is scary.
I'm supposed to just, like, give my heart to someone and they could squish it all up.
It's okay that she is. Whatever happens, we'll adapt. Friends are good at that. Remember: we *choose* to be here.
Here.
SQUISH
I know, right? It's terrifying, but you just gotta jump.
I don't know how to jump.
No one knows how to jump, silly.
Are you sure? I mean...I feel like I'm on a pretty tall cliff. Maybe the tallest in the world.

Pfffft, no! I mean, it's a bit harder for you because of the friendship stuff, but it won't be *hard.*

Abby is so cool about everything.
True. She's so cool.

She is.

I cannot believe I'm in this situation crushing on my best friend.
What a grade-A cliché croissant.
AND I lied about Gram!

Yup. Gram.

I'm wasting your study time.

I'm supposed to be your support system, but I'm a mush system.

It's okay.
Though I am really nervous about this test tomorrow. I can't get below a B.

Okay.

Let's get back to work.

hop

I'm nervous.

Me too. Let's be nervous together.
Okay. Deal.

Friday,
November 5th

Why is this so hard??
I mean..."I like you," that's easy enough to say. It just comes out all wrong whenever I'm around her.

I mean, should I write it out? Should I practice it?

I LIKE YOU.
I like you.
I like you.

Enough, Christine.
She's honestly such a good friend that this literally cannot go badly.
Worst-case scenario, she doesn't feel the same way and you guys are still best friends!
Just freaking do it, already.
ZIP

Who shoved a bug up your butt today?
Ugh. I don't know.

I'm sorry. I'm just so confused.
You've been so wrapped up with all of your Little Mermaid concerns that you haven't even heard about my drama.

You have *drama?!*
You never have drama...
Spill it, woman!

Well, you know those guys in my English class? The cute one and the, well...
I believe the term you're looking for is Grumpy Grumperton.

I'm familiar. Please continue.

I just don't even know how I feel anymore. Jorge is cute and seems so sweet... sometimes.
But he hates Fitz—I think because Fitz tried to stop him from copying off my paper once, but that's beside the point.

Anyway, he just wasn't so nice about Fitz and then Fitz took Abby's posters down and then Fitz asked me out completely out of nowhere and I may have mentioned what he did to Abby's posters, but it turns out it wasn't true and I think I hurt his feelings?

But I didn't even know he had feelings? I mean, I guess everyone does...but you know what I mean.

I never thought he liked *me.* I just really don't know what to believe anymore.
Sigh

Umm... I hate to say it, but Mr. Grumpypants might be right. Your dreamboat sounds kind of like a dingleberry. Or maybe a malicious berry.
A berry with ill intent. Something here is suspect.
rolls eyes

I mean,
first of all, this guy is *wayyyy* off base about Abby. She's basically the epitome of all things wonderful in this world wrapped up in a little anxious ball of cute.

Focus, Christine.

Oh, well, second, why is this guy trying to cheat off your paper? Have you given any thought to what that's all about?

SLAM
Yeah...it's a little concerning, I guess. But he's so nice to me, and funny and...shoot. I don't know.

jingle

Well, you've heard my thoughts. This guy sounds like a grade-A fartbag who's up to no good.

He's not a fartbag. I don't think.

Smooch
KISS

I...

I don't want to
hear it.

All I'm saying is you can just tell me. I'm a good judge of character.

I won't admit that until you admit I'm right about Abby.
And then *tell her.*

RING
RING

Speak of the devil.
ABBY SINCLAIR

Weird.

Yeah, no problem. I'm just on my way home. Can you text me the address?
Be there in like fifteen.

ABBY SINCLAIR
Just tell her.
Well...just admit you think Fitz is cute, then. And Jorge is a turdball.

Abby needs a ride home from a study buddy's house. I'll text you later.

Whatever.

Whoa.

2005

What is this humongous place?

It's wild, right?

Oh. Uh. Hi.

Ready to go, Abs?

Oh, I forgot to use the bathroom.
Can I do that before I go?

Sure, you know where it is.

I'm sorry, I didn't know it was your house that I was...getting Abby from.

Her mom had an emergency of some sort so she said a friend was coming.
I didn't know it would be you.
Hah. Yeah, sometimes she calls me if she thinks the bus will take too long.

You're a good friend.
I try.

...

fidget

Would you like a bubbly water?
Oh, sure.

Your house is, um, fancy.

Yeah, it's ridiculous.

Abby and I have been working together on a proposal for the district with the Unicorn Club. It's to make the bathrooms inclusive for all menstruators. But Abby and I are drafting the proposal together.
Wait...*that's* what you guys are working on? That's great!

POP

Yeah. I want Hazelton to be a more inclusive place for my little brother. He came out recently, and...I...

Roll

Hey! Kick it here.
Really? I'm dreadfully uncoordinated.

Just try!

SAVED

Nice save!

Are you
Brit?

Um. Yeah.
I heard Fitz talking about you.
You should come play soccer with me. I can help you get better.

She might not want to play soccer with you, knucklehead.

I'm going to be a pro, so I'd be a great teacher.
Maybe I'll take you up on that, but I promise it will be a challenge.
Deal. I like challenges.

Buzz off.

I have a little sister. I get wanting to make their lives better.

It's what big siblings are for, right?
We won't be at Hazelton together so I just don't want him to be bullied when I can't be there... With him being trans, well, I want him to be safe.
I love that.

And I love that you're working with Abby on this.

Yeah. Abby's great.
sniff

Hey, Fitz. I think...

Yes?
I think I was wrong. About you, I mean. I feel bad for saying what I said the other day... I'm sorry.
Oh, don't worry about that...

Water under the bridge. But thank you.

Thanks, bud.
slap

Yup.
See you at the Unicorn Club.

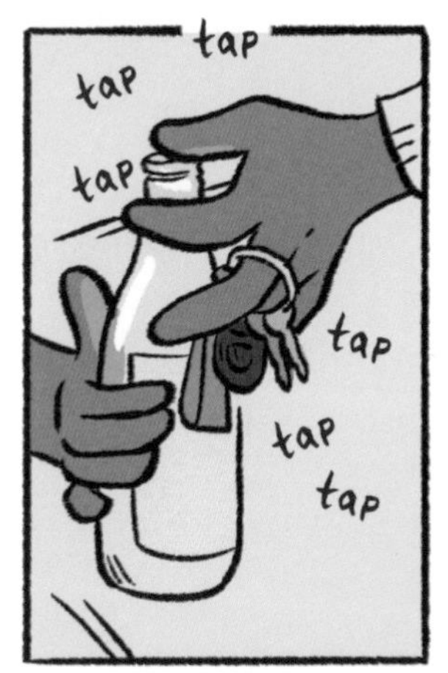
tap
tap
tap
tap
tap
tap

Well...maybe we can study for English again sometime soon?
I'd really like that.

Okay. I'll text you.

So how did my plan of last-minute peeing work?
You did that on purpose?

Oh please, Brit. Of course I did.
All he can talk about besides our proposal is English and working with you. He thinks he's so subtle.

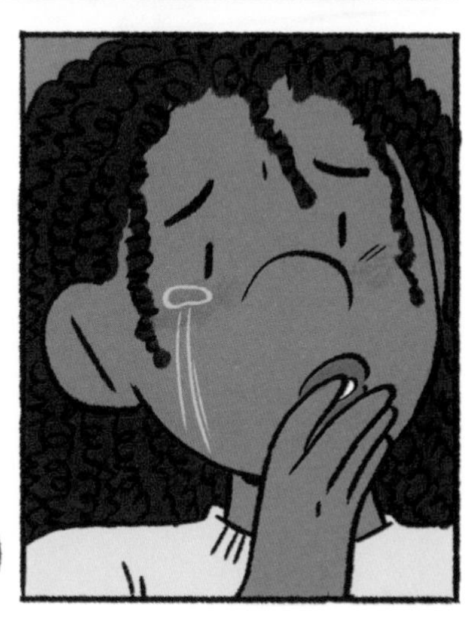

Brit.

I've been so naive.

I thought Jorge was cute and...
...Fitz was just stubborn... and a jerk.

Happens to the best of us.

Christine and I saw Jorge kissing a freshman today.

That fartbag. That's practically an infant.

I know.

Monday, November 8th

H_2O

sniff

Did Mr. Collins explain anything else about the hierarchal structure in class?

Not really, but I'd venture a guess it will be on the test.

nods

blushing

Jorge is dating a freshman.

sniff

Poor girl.

Indeed.

Friday, November 12th

Christine. This is your chance.

toss

Go get 'em!
gulp

Tell her,
just tell her.

You deserve
to be happy.

Who knows what could happen.

It could be good.

Just be your honest self.

I'm gay and
I really like you.
The principal agreed
to stock all the
bathrooms!

...

Huh?
Oh my god.

Wait, can you explain?

Congratulations on all the bathrooms! That's huge!

Thanks, but no... what you said.
Well, I...

I'm gay.

Hey! That's great! I'm so happy for you!

Thank you?

quivers
I wanted to tell you in a better way, and I wanted to...

I don't know...
I'm gay. I'm gay
and I like you.
But I *like*-like
you. I like
you as more
than a friend.
I like you
as a...
I don't know.

Oh.

This is humiliating.
No, it's not.
It's not. I just. I don't have an answer.

Should I have an answer?

I guess not.

I feel weird. Like my stomach is full of bees. Chaotic ones.
bzz
bzz
bzz
I shouldn't have said anything.

I want to know.
We're best friends.
No, you absolutely should have.

You always say we're friends.
We are.
Yeah.
We're friends first.

But do you think it could ever be something...else?
I think I need time to just think about it. Can I have time?

Yes. Absolutely. Please.
What if we met tomorrow and got froyo?
I definitely won't be able to eat and talk about this.
You can always eat.
I want to do whatever the opposite of eating is right now.
Gross.
Tomorrow though? What about the park in the morning? So I can lie on the grass with what's left of my dignity.
Okay, park sounds good. I'll text you.
Deal.

Well, bye.

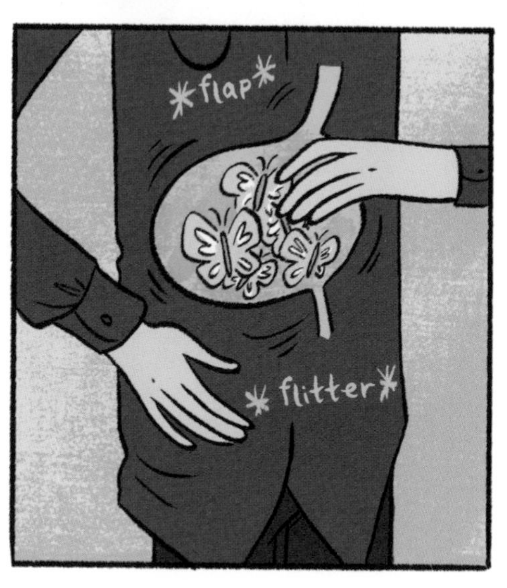
flap
flitter

Well?!

click

click

I feel like a
pile of poop.

Later that night
I feel humiliated.
What if maybe she actually likes me and we could date?
What do we do now?
In third grade she told me we should just get married because boys are stinky.
Should I pretend it was a joke?
What if she thinks today was just stupid?

What will Brit and Sasha think?
Am I gay too if I want to kiss her?
She's cute.
What do we do now?
But we're best friends.
Last year at prom... we danced and it felt so perfect.

Saturday, November 13th

click

click

Hi, sweetie pie.
Why are you so chipper at 9 a.m.?

It's a beautiful sunny Saturday and I had a burst of inspiration, so I wanted to go paint.
click

sigh

What's not to be chipper about?

click
Christine came out to me yesterday.

Good for her!

But she said she *like*-liked me.
Oh, honey. How do you feel about that?

I think I like it.

You know, I had a girlfriend or two in my time.
Hold on. You did?

I did. Sexuality isn't set in stone.
Oat milk, my darling.

Oat

Take a sip.

Are you telling me you're bi?

I never put a label on it. I liked the people I was with so I dated them.
Do you think Christine is attractive?

I do.

I think I've always thought she was cute.

And she's so sweet and smart.
She is. She's such a goof.

Go with your heart.

Croissants from Millies.
millies

I don't think I can eat right now.

I was really thrown off guard by what you said yesterday.

But that's not a bad thing!
PULL

Yeah. Sorry.
You just surprised me!

It's fine.
I don't really know how to tell you how I feel either, so I can imagine.
What I'm saying is that...well... you had to think about this a long time and...

Is there even a right way to say any of this?
Hah, I know.
I mean, like, I have the perfect setup to tell you how I feel right here right now and I'm nervous and I ate, like, three croissants already because I'm really stinking nervous.
I already said *nervous*. But I am!
And I think about you. I mean, I've thought about you like that. I think I don't get crushes that easily so I don't really know how to feel about them.
And when I think of you, we're best friends, you know? So I think I do like you as more than a friend.
I think I just don't know what I am.
That's okay. You don't need to know.

I really know who I am in a lot of ways, but I don't know where I am right now on this.
You do?
But I know I like you.

I don't want to pressure you to do anything or feel anything... Like, this isn't your—well, you see, you don't need to—I just like you and you don't need to like me—
Don't be silly, of course I do.

peck

I wanted to try it.
That's...fine with me.

I think you're cute.
I think you're cute.

Do you want to just, like, see what happens?

I really do.

I don't know how to navigate this.
Me neither. But your friendship is more important to me than anything.

Same. Can we always be friends, no matter what?
Promise.

Millie's

sigh

So...do you have any chocolate croissants in there?

Millie
I thought as much. Here.

Mmm

Thursday, November 18th

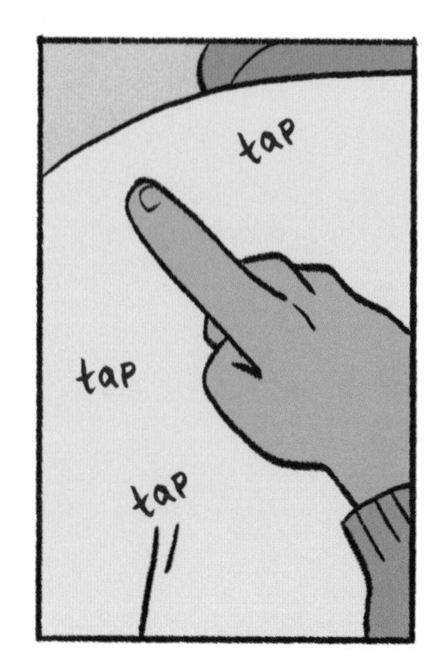
tap
tap
tap

tap
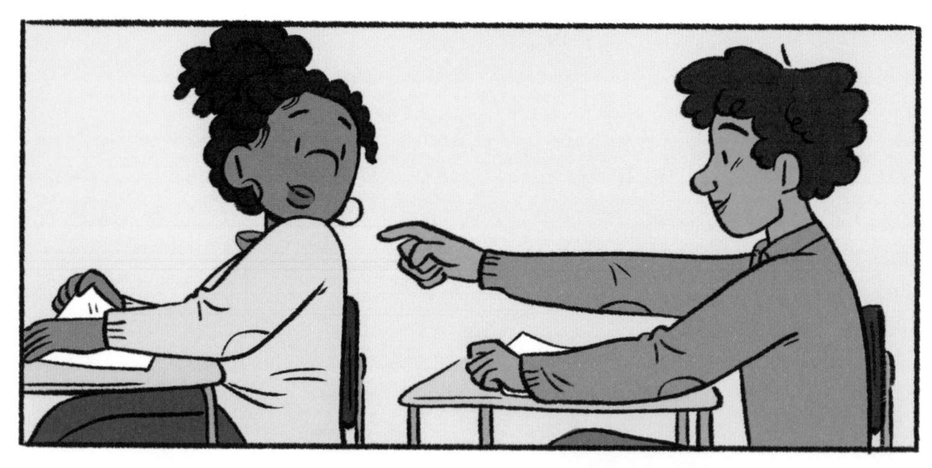

100%

100%

* giggle *

Like I was saying...

Brit, why don't you explain the opening scene of *Emma*?

Okay!

ACHOOOO!

Well...

We make a good team.

I agree.
We could name our team if you want.

Like what? The Study Buddies?

The Book Club?

I was thinking more like maybe calling you my girlfriend.

Oh.

And you could call me your boyfriend.
If you want to.

I'd like that.

Me too.

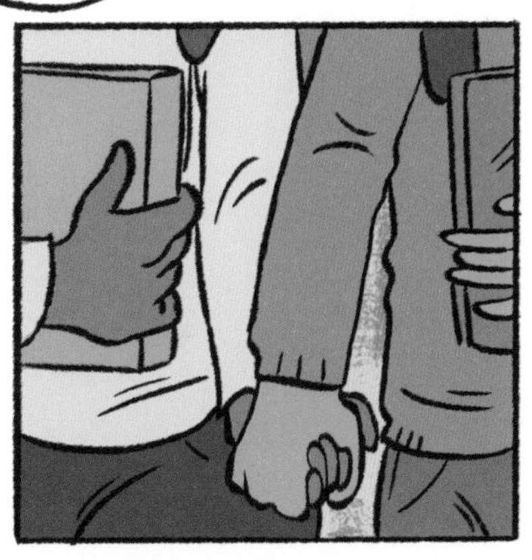

Friday,
November 26th

As and Bs across the board.

Way to go!

You did it.

I was really worried I wouldn't be able to do it.

We knew you could. Let's keep working on that confidence thing...because we know how great you are. You should too.

Yeah, I'm figuring that out.

It takes a lifetime.

I think I want to be a lawyer.

Really? What started this?
A little bit of Elle Woods, but also a bit of me...
I think I'm good at coming up with arguments and seeing all sides of an issue.

Our fights prove this to be true.

I also want to change the world.

I feel like I could make a difference with this. I'm going to join the debate club next semester, and it might take up more of my time, but I want you to know that I'm going to work hard to keep my grades up.

I need them up so I can get into a good undergrad program.
Just let us know what we can do to support you.

Okay, I will.

Saturday,
November 27th

stretch

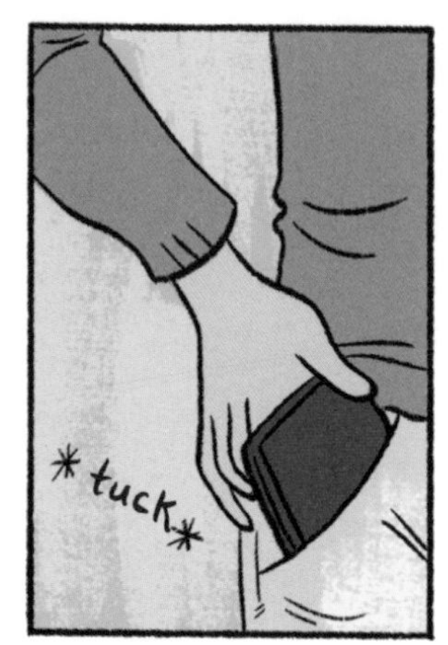
tuck

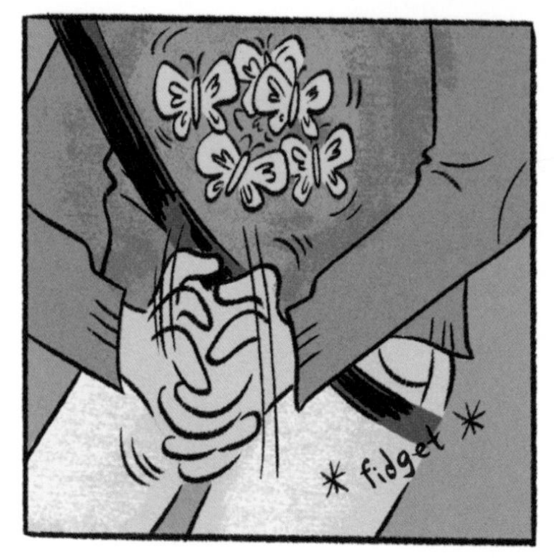
fidget

tug

Hi, Christine.
Hi, Gram!

Bye, Gram!
Frozen
YOGURT

jingle

hmmm...

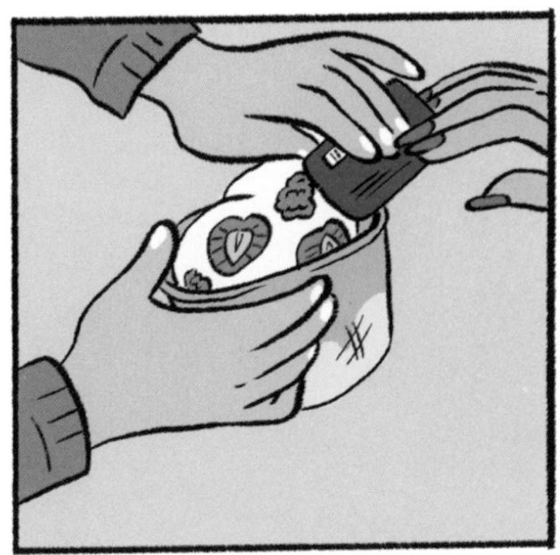

Do you want to sit here?
OPEN

I'm nervous. Can we just walk and eat?

Okay.

I don't know
how to do this.
Me neither.

Do you know how many
times I tried to tell you?
No?

A lot...*a lot*
a lot.

ha
ha
ha

Were you really going to the LGBT club to learn?
At first, yeah.
I met Fitz, and we started working on all our bathroom stuff for the school with the other Unicorns.

It's so cool you all got that passed and the bathrooms will be fully stocked now.

I know, right? I just hope people are respectful about it...

They'll learn. Even if they aren't too cool about it now.

But like,
I was going because of that. Then I realized I just fit in somewhere in there and it gave me a lot to think about.

Holy cannoli, Abs. I had no idea you were going through that!

Would you be cool if I think all sorts of people are cute?

I don't care who you think is cute as long as you think I am.

I really need to go back to the club though.

Come with me again this week! It's really fun. Everyone is so nice, and Fitz is always there too.
Okay. Deal.

Can they handle this much swag though?

I'm sure they won't be able to.

Sunday,
December 5th

Here's to Sasha's good grades!

And bright future!

Thank you, guys.
I think I'm going to kill it on debate team next semester and keep these grades up!
There'll be no arguing with you going forward.

That's the hope!

Thank you.

So how's the new man, Brit?

Um. Cute.

Yes. Good start.

I have something.

I might have agreed to start seeing this cute girl.
But you guys know her so I want to make sure we don't feel awkward.

WHO?

She's this tall drink of water you all know and love.

SQUEALING

I want to die.

Why?
I don't want anyone knowing I like you or you like me.

You only complained about this crush for a million years.
Yeah, I think we already knew.

We promise to put our friendship first and not make it weird.

You make everything weird.
True.

Fair.
But you know what I mean. I just...don't want you to like... you know...

We dont want to jeopardize the friendship we have with you guys or each other.

I love that, but also let things figure themselves out and we'll make it work.
So wise.

mmm

I feel like a weight's been lifted off my chest having said that.

You didn't say that. I said that.
Yeah but you said it *for* me.
You can't even wait five blocks to dig into your leftovers?

Seriously. Why do you even bother packing them up?

They were getting sad and I didn't want them to be alone. So now they're in my belly with their friends.
You're ridiculous.

I'm a powerful machine. I need a continuous supply of fuel.

CRAFT ST
ha
ha
ha

Hi, Mom!

ahhh

I brought self-care.

Much appreciated.

ACHOOO!!
Do NOT infect me. I'm warning you!

I won't. Fitz got over his cold in like three days. I'm fine.

muah
muah

shove

You're one to talk.

Let's not discuss this here.
Where else should we discuss it?

shrug

Chips

Chips

Ooh! Are these the face masks with animals printed on them?

Yes! They are!

GASP
That's disrespectful to rabbits everywhere.

Ooh, I need one of those too.

SPLAT

Frog on your face, frog in my throat.
!
ha ha ha

Are we going to watch this thing already?

I'd personally like to know when we are allowed to watch a different movie.

Never.

I'm with them. Brit's turned me around on this. Darcy is life.

Not you too!

Click

Click

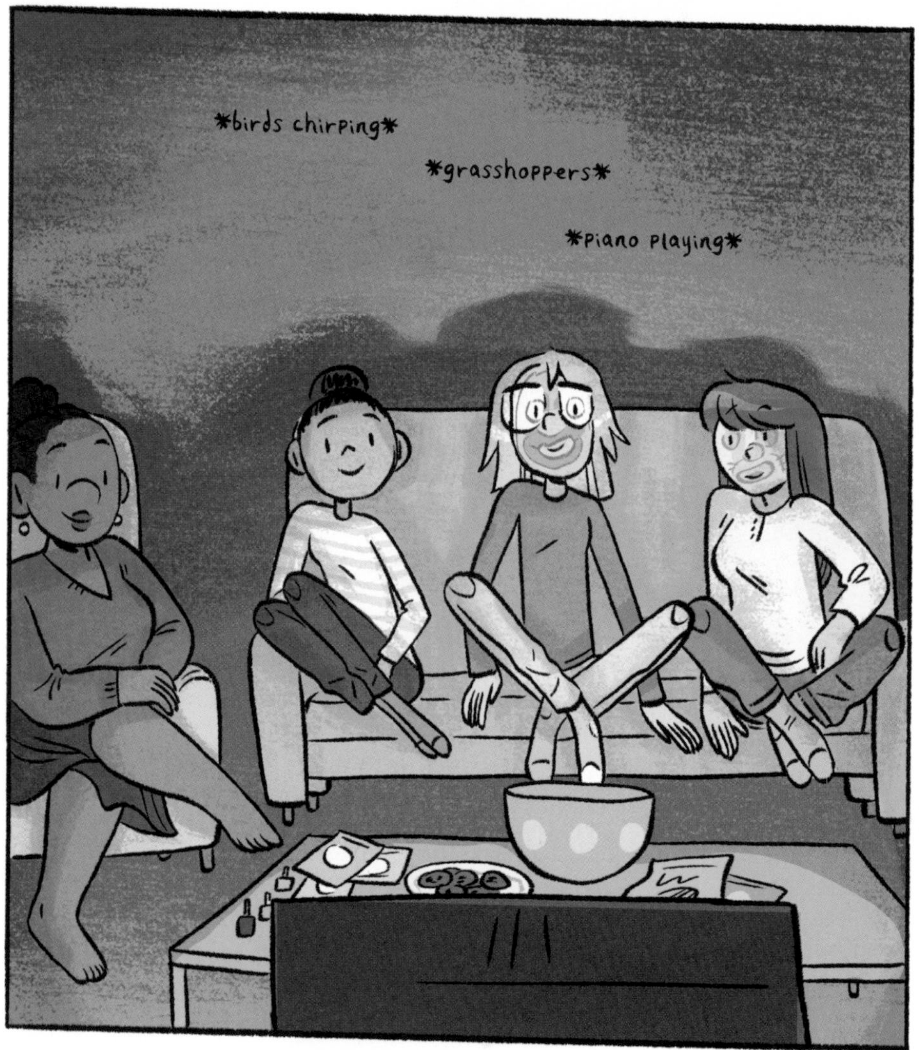
birds chirping
grasshoppers
piano playing

Lydia, Kitty!
Okay. I guess
I like it too.

Shhh.

Authors' Note

When we made *Go with the Flow,* we wanted to tell a story about friendship centered around periods for kids, tweens, and teens. In that graphic novel, we showed readers periods and the struggles around them clearly in drawings, without shame and without hiding the bloodiness in metaphor. Even when we wrote *Go with the Flow*, we knew what would happen in the sequel, *Look on the Bright Side.* What we didn't know, though, was if the world had room in it for a visual story that dealt with periods. Thankfully for us and our readers, the world needed it! *Go with the Flow* said almost everything we could about periods. For everything we left out, we put it in *Look on the Bright Side.*

The reality of having a period is that many different people menstruate. Girls, women, trans men, nonbinary people, gender-nonconforming people, intersex people, rich people, poor people, people with disabilities, and people without access to adequate hygiene menstruate. Menstruation is something most women and girls experience, and because of that, we often talk about it through that lens and from the perspective of people who can afford to menstruate. However, people who were assigned female at birth but identify otherwise also experience menstruation. Any way you identify, if you menstruate, understand that it is nothing to be ashamed of but rather something to accept and embrace as part of being human.

Identity comes in all sorts of forms. Throughout our lives we are on a never-ending search to find who we are. Who you are is an ever-changing thing, fluid and encouraged forward by life events that change you. From life's wins to life's losses, we are always growing and changing. There is so much beauty in each of us and our unique makeups. However you find yourself in this world at this moment, we hope you have the support system you need around you. If it hasn't been provided for you, we hope that it can be found through friendships and communities that build you up.

We can't control the life that's given to us. We see that through Brit's struggles with her endometriosis and Christine's struggles to open up about her identity. However, we can choose what we do with the life we are given. We can work to make the world more kind and inclusive at home (like Sasha's parents encouraging her to find her path) and in the world around us (like Abby, who works with her community to make the world more accessible for her peers). Leaving the world a kinder and gentler place is something we can all do in many ways...but mostly we can do it by being good to the people around us.

Thank you for picking up this story and trusting us again with our beloved characters Abby, Brit, Christine, and Sasha—who would probably be pretty thrilled to know how many people love them. We know that we feel the same.

Love always,

Lily and Karen

Acknowledgments

This book would not have been possible without the many amazing people who helped it become realized from start to finish.

Thank you to Emily Feinberg for believing in us from the start. To Minju Chang, who supported our vision. To Emilia Sowersby for your feedback and enthusiasm. To Molly Johanson for your impeccable taste. Thank you to Kirk Benshoff for your direction. To Sarah Gompper for your organization. To Alexa Blanco for your big-picture vision. To Molly Brouillette and the entire Macmillan marketing team that helped this book even come into existence. To the Macmillan schools and library team for your grade-A enthusiasm. To Anah Tillar, Anna Poon, and River Kai for your honest and unflinching feedback. Thank you, all!

Thank you to Kaley Bales for your incredible color direction and work ethic that brought vibrancy and life to this book.

Lily would like to thank her entire family: Thank you for always letting me complain about my periods and for all their support before, during, and after my endometriosis surgery and health battles. Thank you to my amazing husband, C. Grey Hawkins, for absolutely everything...but also for reminding me to go step outside and get some fresh air. To my mom and dad for always encouraging my inner Abby. To Paige, Lucy, Kaley, Larissa, Emily, Vicky, Bel, Raina, Laura, and more for your wonderful supportive friendships. To all my doctors whose help allowed this book to be worked on at rapid speed, especially Dr. Dale. And of course, to Karen, for embarking on this journey with me and being the best cocreator anyone could hope for!

Karen would like to thank her parents, John and Laurie, her husband, Ryan, and her two amazing little humans, Alex and Jakob: Thank you for supporting me in all my strange ideas and interests no matter how absurd they sometimes sound. Thank you also to all my friends and extended family for all the laughs and for encouraging me to reveal my inner Christine. And finally, thank you to Lily, my feminist collaborator, without whom none of this would have been possible. I'm forever grateful to you for helping me survive our middle school presentations, the very thought of which still give me anxiety.

A huge monumental thank-you goes out to all the booksellers who hand-sold *Go with the Flow* throughout the COVID-19 pandemic, helping make this sequel a possibility. Thank you to all the librarians who've fought for our books to be accessible and read by those who need them. To the teachers who put this book on the shelves of their classrooms for easy access and no judgment. To the parents and guardians who got this book for their kids and read it with them.

And thank YOU, dear reader, for picking up our books and enjoying Abby, Brit, Christine, and Sasha's adventures at Hazelton High.

Lily Williams is the author and illustrator of the If Animals Disappeared series, including *If Sharks Disappeared*, *If Bees Disappeared*, and *If Tigers Disappeared*, as well as *Go With the Flow*. She grew up in Northern California where she received her BFA from California College of the Arts before moving to Colorado. Lily seeks to inspire change, engage audiences, and educate people of all ages with her artwork. Her work can be seen in films and books and on the web at **lilywilliamsart.com**.

Karen Schneemann grew up in Northern California. She received her first undergraduate degree in engineering from UCLA and her second in animation from California College of the Arts. In addition to being an engineer, artist, and writer, Karen is also a mom to two adorable kids. She lives and works in foggy San Francisco, California.

We dedicate this book to all who have struggled
to find their place in this world.
—Lily and Karen

Published by First Second
First Second is an imprint of Roaring Brook Press,
a division of Holtzbrinck Publishing Holdings Limited Partnership
120 Broadway, New York, NY 10271
firstsecondbooks.com

Library of Congress Control Number: 2022920397

First edition, 2023
Edited by Emily Feinberg
Jacket design and interior design by Molly Johanson
Production editing by Sarah Gompper

Penciled with Blackwing pencils. Inked and colored digitally in Photoshop.

Printed in China by RR Donnelley Asia Printing Solutions Ltd., Dongguan City, Guangdong Province

ISBN 978-1-250-83410-2 (paperback)
10 9 8 7 6 5 4 3 2 1

ISBN 978-1-250-83411-9 (hardcover)
10 9 8 7 6 5 4 3 2 1